NICKELODEON

Drake & Josh

NICKELODEON

Drake & Josh

Blues Brothers

By Laurie McElroy
Based on "Blues Brothers," written by CRAIG DIGREGORIO
and "Number One Fan," written by DAN SCHNEIDER

Based on *Drake and Josh*, created by DAN SCHNEIDER

SCHOLASTIC INC.
New York   Toronto   London   Auckland   Sydney
Mexico City   New Delhi   Hong Kong   Buenos Aires

No part of this publication may be reproduced in whole or in part, stored in a retrieval system, or transmitted in any form or by any means, electronic, mechanical, photocopying, recording, or otherwise, without written permission of the publisher. For information regarding permission, write to Scholastic Inc., Attention: Permissions Department, 557 Broadway, New York, NY 10012.

ISBN 0-439-83162-8

Published by Scholastic Inc. All rights reserved.
SCHOLASTIC and associated logos are trademarks and/or registered trademarks of Scholastic Inc.

12 11 10 9 8 7 6 5 4 3 2 1   6 7 8 9 10/0

Printed in the U.S.A.

First printing, March 2006

Part One:
Blues Brothers

Prologue

Drake Parker sat on his bed, shuffling a deck of cards. "When I was a little kid, my mom told me I have a lucky star."

Josh Nichols hung out in the living room, playing with a paddle ball. "I sweat when I sleep," he said, making a face. Even he had to admit, it was kind of gross.

"I guess Mom was right. It's like I always win stuff, even when I don't try," Drake said with a shrug.

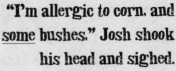

"I'm allergic to corn, and some bushes." Josh shook his head and sighed.

Drake's mom was totally right — he had always been lucky. "In fourth grade, I won class president..."

"If I even sniff the wrong shrub, my head swells up like a melon." Josh added.

"...and I didn't even run for class president," Drake said.

Josh tried to hit the ball with the paddle. He missed. "Fourth grade? Not a good year for the Joshie."

Drake listed some of the other lucky things that happened to him in fourth grade. "Then I won some music competition, the hundred yard dash, best hair ..."

Josh shook his head sadly, thinking about the fourth grade. "I used to get really nervous in school."

"... I won a rabbit in the fair. Not sure how," Drake said. "Nice bunny. I named him George."

"Once, I was supposed to take a spelling test, so I actually hid under my bed." Josh remembered. "I got stuck."

"I entered George into a rabbit contest. <u>He</u> won," Drake chuckled.

"They had to use power tools to get me out from under the bed." Josh made a face. "And lotion."

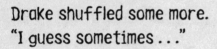

Drake shuffled some more. "I guess sometimes..."

"Things just don't always go the way you want them to." Josh missed the ball again.

"Things just work out the way you want them to." Drake leaned back with a confident smile.

Josh popped open a can of soda. It sprayed all over his face. He sputtered and waved his arms in frustration, as if to say, "<u>See</u>, things don't go the way you want them to."

Drake popped open a soda and took a satisfying sip. "Ahh."

CHAPTER ONE

"Good morning, San Diego," Josh announced, walking into the kitchen.

His stepbrother, Drake, and stepsister, Megan, were eating breakfast at the table.

Josh grabbed the orange juice and held it up next to his face. "Today's forecast: partly orange juice." He grabbed a couple of pancakes from a plate on the counter and waved them around. "With a thirty percent chance of pancakes. And look out, it's going to be *raining syrup!*"

Drake ignored him. He was pretty used to his brother acting totally goofy.

Drake and Josh were two guys with two different — totally different — personalities. Going to the same school used to be the only thing they had in common, but that changed in a huge way when Josh's dad married Drake and Megan's mom. Drake and Josh were suddenly brothers — and roommates.

Not that Drake was what you would call happy

about it at first. Drake was totally into having a good time — playing his guitar and hanging with his friends. He wasn't exactly big on school — well, except for the girls — and he'd rather do anything than homework. He thought Josh was more than a little strange, in an especially geeky sort of way.

Josh was totally into following the rules — *all* the rules. Teachers thought he was the greatest. Not only did he do all his homework and study for tests, Josh did extra credit assignments, too. In other words, Josh didn't exactly hang with the same high school in-crowd as Drake did.

But hanging with his cool new stepbrother was one of Josh's favorite things to do. And Drake learned to like having Josh around — most of the time.

"Raining syrup!" Josh said again, squeezing the syrup bottle over his pancakes.

Drake and Megan looked at each other and rolled their eyes. Josh wasn't going to stop until they asked him what was up with his weather-themed breakfast.

"Say, Josh." Drake stood and went to get more pancakes. "Is there a reason you're acting *extra* weird today?"

Josh grinned. "You're not going to be calling me *extra* weird when everyone sees me on the six o'clock news tonight."

"Why are you going to be on the news?" Drake headed to the refrigerator for the butter. "Did you get yourself locked in the monkey cage at the zoo again?"

"Hey!" Josh put his hands on his hips. "Those chimps tricked me! The big one stole my corn dog." He turned to Megan. "I mean, I had to go in there and get it back!" Josh knew when to take a stand. No chimp was going to get the better of him, especially when a corn dog was involved.

Megan giggled. She loved it when Josh acted like a total goofball. He was so good at it. Of course, every now and then she'd help him to look like one, but a lot of the time, he'd do it by himself.

Josh turned back to Drake. "And I'd do it again," he said with an emphatic nod of his head. "Anyway," Josh said, sitting down with his breakfast plate. "It's Junior Anchor Day at Dad's TV station and he picked me to be the weatherboy to his weatherman."

Josh's dad, Walter Nichols, was the weatherman at KDLY, San Diego's most popular local news station.

Josh was always cracking up at his dad's jokes. Drake and Megan thought their stepdad was a great guy, but when it came to his corny jokes, they weren't exactly rolling on the floor laughing.

Josh's TV news got Megan's attention. "*You're* going to be on TV with Dad?"

"That's right!" Josh announced proudly.

Megan stabbed her waffle with a fork. "I can't believe he picked you instead of me." If anyone deserved to be on TV with Dad, it was her, not this big goof of a brother.

Drake stood at the kitchen counter, ignoring the discussion. How could he think about tonight's news with all these breakfast choices in front of him now? He held a waffle in one hand and a pancake in the other, trying to decide which was tastier. Then he had an awesome idea. "I wonder if there's a way to merge the waffle with the pancake," he said to himself.

Megan zeroed in on Josh through narrowed eyes. "I'm going to talk to Dad about this," she said.

Drake put the waffle on top of the pancake. "You could call it a panfle," he said, tasting his creation.

"No." He grabbed another pancake and made a waffle sandwich. He took a big bite. "The wafcake."

Josh felt bad that Megan was upset, but he wasn't about to give up his chance to be on TV. Dad could bring Megan next time. "C'mon, don't be jealous, Megan," Josh said. "Your time will come."

Megan glared at him. "And so will yours, Josh. So. Will. Yours," she said slowly, staring right into his eyes. She grabbed her plate and stalked out of the kitchen.

Josh was worried. He'd seen that look in Megan's eyes before, and it scared him. Megan looked like a cute little girl dressed in pink with her big dark eyes and long dark hair pinned back with flower clips. But she gave new meaning to the word "troublemaker." She loved pulling pranks on Drake and Josh, and stopped at nothing to embarrass her brothers.

"What did she mean by that?" he asked Drake. Drake had lived with Megan and her scary pranks for a lot longer than Josh had. Maybe he had some special insight.

"I don't know, but if I were you I'd sleep with a helmet on." Drake took another bite of his wafcake. You would think Drake would know how to read his little sister by now, but with Megan you could never be sure what she was up to. At least now he had Josh around to share the pain.

For Josh, it wasn't raining syrup anymore. It was raining worry.

CHAPTER TWO

Later that day in study hall, Drake wandered over to the bulletin board.

It was covered with flyers and posters for Belleview High School clubs and teams. He pulled out a pen to add his name to one of the sign up sheets.

Josh followed and sat on a desk. "Hey, if you're signing up for the Physics Club, you're too late," he said. He wore a blue-flowered Hawaiian shirt over a bright red T-shirt and his dark brown hair was neat, like always. "All the cool spots are taken." Josh had signed up just in time to be treasurer.

Drake wore what he always wore — in or out of school — faded jeans with a vintage logo T-shirt. His shaggy brown hair covered his forehead as he stared at Josh in disbelief. "Okay, first of all, there aren't any *cool* spots in the Physics Club," Drake said. "Besides, I'm signing up for the talent show." He pointed to the poster that read, "Belleview Talent Contest."

"Oh, awesome," Josh said. "You know it's at the Premiere this year." The Premiere was the movie theater and café where Josh worked after school and on weekends. Half the school hung out there.

"Oh, I know," Drake said.

"Hey, didn't you win last year?" Josh asked.

"Actually —"

A pretty girl with curly brown hair rushed up, cutting off Drake's answer. "He won last year and the year before!" she said. "That's two years in a row! And when he wins this year, that'll be a three-peat!" she squealed.

Drake and Josh exchanged confused looks.

"Do I know you?" Drake asked.

"No," she smiled shyly. "I love you. 'Bye."

Josh watched the girl run away. Pretty girls certainly didn't rush up to him like that and say, "I love you" — not when he was awake, anyway. But it happened to Drake all the time. Josh turned to his brother. "It's got to be fun being you."

Drake started to disagree, but then he thought about it for a minute. It *was* fun being him. "Yeah," he answered.

A guy wearing an argyle sweater-vest and short sleeve shirt walked over. He looked Drake up and down with a sneer. "I wouldn't count on winning the talent contest this year if I were you, Drake," he said.

"Oh yeah?" Drake turned and matched the guy's sneer. "Who's going to beat me, Hewitt?" Drake spat the name as if even forming the word in his mouth made him sick.

Hewitt snapped his fingers. In an instant four boys surrounded him, all of them with super-neat hair and clothes — just like Hewitt's.

"We are," Hewitt said.

"Hey, aren't you guys in the chorus?" Josh asked.

"Choral *Society*," Hewitt corrected. "And we rock!" He pumped his fist in the air.

"Oh yeah," Drake said sarcastically. "You guys really *rocked* our front porch with those Christmas carols last year."

"Oh, yeah! Didn't you guys do an a capella version of 'Silent Night'?" Josh smiled, remembering. He loved Christmas carols.

"You mean like this?" Hewitt signaled his crew.

They launched into their harmonized version of the Christmas song — it was as far from rocking as Alaska is from Florida. But they did sound great. They sang on key, tight. It was almost perfect.

> *Silent night, holy night. All is calm, all is bright,*
> *'Round yon virgin, mother and child.*

Josh couldn't help himself. Even though Hewitt was Drake's archenemy, at that moment Josh just had to sing along. His high, off-key voice didn't exactly blend in with the Choral Society.

> *Holy infant so tender and mild*

The Choral Society stopped singing and stared angrily at Josh. How dare he ruin their perfect harmony?

> *Sleep in heavenly peeeee-eeeaaace*

Josh suddenly realized that he was singing alone,

and finished the song under his breath before sliding into his desk. "Sleepinheavenlypeace."

Drake and Hewitt glared at each other. They were in agreement on one thing — the talent show challenge was on.

CHAPTER THREE

Drake knew his rock band was better than Hewitt's Choral Society any day. But he still needed to practice. After school he headed to his bedroom where he put on his headphones and played his electric guitar.

Before Josh moved in, Drake's bedroom had been his own private paradise. It was kind of unfinished, with exposed beams and unpainted wallboard, but Drake liked it that way. He built a loft bed under the window, bought an old couch and comfy chairs at a yard sale, and filled the walls with all kinds of cool posters, road signs, and old license plates. It was a young bachelor's dream. There was nothing better than kicking back on the couch, his feet up on the coffee table, and watching the tube or playing video games.

Then Josh moved in.

Drake wasn't exactly thrilled to have to share his space at first. They both wanted the loft bed, but there was no way Drake was giving that up. Josh got the couch — he even had to sleep in the bathtub once.

But then they added a bed for Josh, and Drake had to admit that it was easier to find things with a neat guy like Josh around — plus Josh had a better stereo system.

Still, there were times — like now when Drake needed to focus on his music — that sharing a room with Josh could be kind of a pain.

Josh sat on the couch next to Drake, and started to check his weather charts. He only had two more hours to prepare for his debut as San Diego's junior weatherman. Then he headed to the window with a huge weather thermometer and hung outside to check the temperature. But the house next door was blocking his view, and Josh couldn't get a good look at the sky. He leaned forward until almost half of his body was hanging out of the window, and then —

The window dropped with a thump and hit him in the back.

Josh was pinned!

He thrashed around trying to get Drake's attention. The top half of his body hung out of the window — two stories up. His bottom half was still in his bedroom, but his feet couldn't touch the floor. He kicked his legs wildly behind him, hitting nothing but air. He was like a giant teeter-totter, but he couldn't move up or down.

Drake was too absorbed in his music to notice. His headphones blocked the sound of Josh calling for help.

"Drake! Drake!" Josh yelled. "Stuck in the window!" Josh's legs flailed behind him. Drake still didn't notice. Was he going to be stuck here forever? What if the neighbors saw him? Mrs. Johnson already crossed the street whenever she saw him coming. But could Josh help it if her little white poodle happened to walk by just when he was having a leg spasm? Fluffy had hardly been hurt, but she still yapped like crazy whenever Josh walked by the house.

Finally, after what seemed like hours of wild flailing, Josh managed to kick the desk chair. It rolled into the back of Drake's chair.

Drake jumped and pulled his headphones off. "Not again," he muttered. He grabbed the back of Josh's jeans with one hand and tried to prop open the window with the other. "Suck it in, Josh! C'mon!" Drake yelled.

"Sucking!" Josh gasped.

Drake pulled. Josh sucked. Drake gritted his teeth and pulled harder.

That was enough to drag Josh loose. They both fell back into the bedroom, and the window came down with a slam. Josh hit the floor. The force pushed Drake into the side of his loft bed with a bang.

Josh jumped to his feet. "I'm okay," he said, panting. "I'm okay."

"Okay, that's the *last* time I'm pulling you back in," Drake warned.

"Sorry." Josh went back to his weather charts as if nothing had happened. "I was checking the sky for signs of precipitation. I'm going to be on TV in two hours and I want my forecast to be up to the minute. You know, weather is a very complex science."

Drake rolled his eyes and moved away. Josh had a habit of getting really into things like weather and magic tricks.

Josh kept talking. He had learned a lot about weather from his dad. "See, before there was radar, the mariners used to use the sky to forecast if there was going to be thunderstorms, lightning storms —"

The bedroom door slammed. Drake was *not* going to sit and listen to the history of weather when he had a talent show to practice for.

"Okay," Josh called out. "I'll tell you later, Drake." Josh understood; not everyone could think weather was as exciting as he did.

He headed toward the mirror and cleared his throat before practicing his TV delivery. "Today's FORECAST," he said with a big grin. "TODAY'S forecast . . . Today's FOREcast . . . Today's foreCAST."

Megan crawled out from under Josh's bed, where she had been hiding, waiting for this moment. Her face popped up in the mirror behind him. "Boo!" she said.

"*Aaaarrgggbhh!*" Josh screamed, clutching his chest. "What? You want me to have a stroke?"

"Sure." She laughed. "Go ahead." Scaring Josh was just too easy.

Josh tried to make her feel better about the whole TV thing — maybe she'd call off whatever horrible prank she had planned. "Look, Megan. I know why you're upset."

"Do you?" Megan asked.

"Yeah, because Dad didn't pick you to be on TV," Josh said.

"I don't care." Megan shrugged.

She sounded convincing, but Josh didn't believe her. Here's the thing about Megan: She *always* had an ulterior motive. Like the time she folded the laundry and slipped itching powder into all his underpants. Or the time she pretended to be interested in the medieval catapult he built for school, and then used it to project rotten tomatoes at him at fifty miles per hour. Since when didn't Megan care about Josh getting to be on TV with Dad instead of her? "You don't care?" he asked.

"Nope." Megan walked casually around the room. She picked up a snow globe and shook it. "I don't want to be on TV."

"Why not?" Josh still didn't trust her. What was she up to?

"I'd be way too scared," Megan said.

"Really?" Josh asked. Megan scared? This was a whole new side of her. "I'm not scared at all."

"Wow! I sure would be if I knew *millions* of people

would be watching me." Megan smiled and played with a bobble-head doll. "On *live* TV." She put the doll down and got serious. "That's pressure."

Josh swallowed. "Pressure?" His voice cracked. Pressure was not something he did well with.

"Serious pressure," Megan said, stressing the word "serious" as she walked toward Josh. "I mean, think about it. You make one mistake, and millions of people will see it. That's almost like making millions of mistakes — in front of the *whole* world."

"I never thought about that." Josh gulped. Millions of people, watching him.

"Yeah, well, I'm sure you'll be fine." Megan laughed, then got serious again. She stared right into Josh's eyes. "Unless your twitch comes back."

"What twitch?" Josh asked.

"The one with your face," Megan said innocently. "Remember the fourth grade, Josh? The twitch?" she pressed. "Whenever you got nervous?"

Josh's eyes got wide. How did Megan know? Their parents had only been married a year. He didn't even know Megan existed when he was in the fourth grade. "Wait! Who told you I twitched?"

"Dad," Megan answered.

"Dad!" Josh crossed his arms over his chest. He couldn't believe his own father had told Megan about the twitch. Traitor!

"Yeah," Megan answered cheerfully. "Well, have fun on TV!" She skipped out of the room. Her work there was done — it was only a matter of time before Josh had a meltdown.

Josh watched Megan leave, thinking about making millions of mistakes in front of millions of people. He remembered the twitch in fourth grade. How embarrassing it was. How much everyone laughed at him. He didn't see Megan's grin as she left the room, but he knew she was trying to psych him out . . . and it was working.

He shook his head. "So much evil, in such a little girl."

CHAPTER FOUR

Later that evening, Audrey Parker-Nichols entered the family's cozy living room carrying a big bowl of popcorn. She was a cool mom who knew how to have a good time. She worked hard, but her new family came first. Josh's TV appearance was definitely something the whole family could celebrate.

"Drake! Megan!" she called. "Josh is about to be on TV!" Audrey put the popcorn down and grabbed the remote.

Drake ran in, followed by Megan.

"Is he on?" Drake asked.

"In just a second!" Audrey turned up the volume. "How cool is this?" she said. "Your dad and Josh on TV together."

They stopped to listen to the anchorman. "Next we will check in with our meteorologist Walter Nichols. And since it's Junior Anchor Day, our weatherman Walter will be joined by his son, Josh. Walter?"

Audrey was so excited for Josh. Drake just hoped

Josh wouldn't do anything goofy, like knock over the weather map. Megan sat waiting for her plan to work.

Walter stood in front of the weather map. Josh stood stiffly at his side, wearing a tan sports coat with elbow patches, a blue shirt, and a red and white tie.

"Thanks, Stuart," Walter said. "It's another sunny day here in San Diego." Walter was about to point to the weather map, but Josh was in the way. "Son, you're blocking downtown," he said.

"Oh, sorry." Josh stepped to the side and smiled nervously.

"So, Josh, what's the weekend looking like?" Walter asked.

"Well, you might want to take those swim trunks out because it looks like the sunshine is here to stay," Josh said. He pointed to the big yellow suns all over the map and smiled like an old pro.

"That's good news, son," Walter said.

"Hey. Josh is doing really well," Audrey said.

Drake was surprised. Josh was actually pulling it off without making a fool of himself. "He almost makes the weather interesting."

"Yeah." Megan crunched a piece of popcorn. She

knew it was just a matter of time before Josh started twitching. Her plan would work. Her plans *always* worked. "This should be interesting," she said knowingly.

Josh was still gesturing to the weather map. "We've got a warm front coming in from the coast and that's going to merge with this ridge of high pressure. . . ." Josh was demonstrating where the high pressure was on the weather map when suddenly he heard Megan's voice in his head. *"Serious pressure,"* she had said that afternoon.

Josh froze. His eyes darted around like a caged animal. He started to sweat. And sweat. "Uh . . . High . . . High . . . pressure."

He heard Megan's voice again. *"You make one mistake, and millions of people see it."*

Josh stuttered and stammered, trying to remember what he was supposed to say next. All he could think of were the millions of people who were watching him make one mistake after the other.

Walter stared at Josh, trying to figure out what was going on.

"Um . . . the . . . uh . . . the . . . uh the pressure system . . ." Josh babbled.

"Remember the fourth grade, Josh?" Megan's voice whispered in his ear. *"The twitch?"*

Josh's face started to twitch. "Ohhh," he groaned. Actually, it was more than just his face. The twitch started with his right cheek, then moved down his neck, and back to the top of his head. Soon his whole body was involved, jerking one way, then the other.

Audrey and Drake gaped at the TV with open mouths. They were speechless. What was happening to Josh?

Megan watched it all with a big satisfied smile. "How great is this?" she asked.

On the television, Walter's jaw dropped as Josh had a total meltdown — stammering, twitching, and sweating like crazy. He had no idea how to help his son. "Josh, uh, why don't you let me explain to the folks exactly why —"

Josh twitched some more. He was like a life-sized marionette whose puppeteer had lost control of the strings. "Why did you have to tell her about the twitch?" he moaned. Josh turned back to the camera, determined to get through his part of the broadcast. "Um . . . the high pressure system." The twitch had traveled from the right side of his face, down the right side of his body, and then up his left side. His face couldn't even figure out which way to twitch anymore.

"It's a little warm in here," Josh said. He took off his jacket. There were humungous sweat stains under his arms. His light blue shirt was suddenly navy blue. Practically his whole shirt was wet.

"Josh!" Walter was horrified. When Josh twitched in fourth grade it was kind of cute, but now it was a bit embarrassing. He had to stop this disaster.

Josh held his arms out and noticed the huge wet stains. He couldn't stop twitching. "It seems my anti-perspirant has failed," he said with a moan. "Aw, geez!"

Walter quickly turned to the camera. "Well, we all know it's going to be sunny, so let's never speak of this again."

Josh stood behind him, still twitching — now his whole body was practically convulsing!

Walter tried to turn the show over to the anchor-man. "Back to you, Stuart," he said with a stiff smile. But Stuart was too busy cracking up to take back the show. "Stuart," Walter said again, more firmly. "Back. To. You."

Audrey and Drake watched from the couch as Josh gave one last giant, uncontrollable twitch. Megan took it all in with an evil grin. Who knew having a brother like Josh could be so much fun?

CHAPTER FIVE

Drake hung out at one of the Premiere's café tables with his band. The Premiere was a movie theater and also one of the town's local teen hangouts. Since Josh worked there, Drake knew he could always practice there. Plus he could talk Josh into letting him into movies for free once in a while.

Drake played his guitar while his band members drank sodas and took notes.

"So when I get to the part, *if you open up your mind*," Drake sang, "sing the backgrounds on *mind*, okay?"

The guys nodded.

Helen, the tough and sassy manager of the theater and Josh's boss, walked over. She was hard on Josh, but she had a soft spot for Drake. "Drake Parker! So good to see you," she said.

Drake checked out her bright red shirt and dangling earrings. He liked Helen. He could turn on the charm and she'd do him favors — like slipping him free candy when he went to the movies. "Looking good, Helen," Drake said.

"I know." Helen leaned against the back of Drake's chair with a smile. "So what are you boys up to?" she asked.

"Just getting ready for the talent show," Drake answered.

"Oh, you know you're going to win, Drake." Helen waved her hand as if it were a done deal. "You won last year, too, right?"

The same girl from study hall came out of nowhere. Her brown curls bounced up and down as she squealed. "He won last year and the year before! That's two years in a row! And when he wins this year, that'll be a *three-peat*." She giggled. "I love you, Drake."

The girl darted away before Drake could respond.

Helen was as confused by the girl's sudden rush of energy as Drake was. "Who was that?" she asked.

Drake shook his head. "I don't know."

"Hmm. Anyway, have you seen your brother?" Helen checked her watch. "He's ten minutes late for work. And he knows how I feel about tardiness."

"Yeah," Drake said. It wasn't like Josh to be late. When Josh wasn't right on time, it was usually because he was early. "He should be here by now. I don't know —" Drake's cell phone rang. "Sorry. Hang on a second."

"Oh, that's okay, you go right ahead," Helen said. "You look so cute when you talk on your cell phone . . . like a little businessman." She went back to work with a big grin. Drake could get away with pretty much anything when Helen was around. She even once made him manager of the Premiere over Josh, even though Josh did all the work while Drake played video games. There was just something about Drake's shaggy brown hair and cute smile that made Helen want to go easy on him. Josh, on the other hand, was easy to boss around.

"Hello," Drake said into his phone.

Josh popped up from behind a trash can a few feet away. "Drake!" he said into his phone. "C'mere!"

"Hey, you're late for work," Drake said. "Where are you?"

Josh popped his head up again. "Here. Behind the trash can." He ducked and waved his arm in the air.

Drake headed across the room with a confused expression and knelt next to Josh. "Why are you hiding back here?" he said into his phone.

"I'm afraid," Josh answered, still on the phone.

The brothers suddenly realized they were next to each other and flipped their phones closed.

"Afraid of what?" Drake asked.

"People." Josh shuddered, remembering the horrible twitching. "What if they saw me on TV?"

"Dude, no one watches the weather. I guarantee you no one here saw it," Drake said. He didn't really believe that — Josh's meltdown was the kind of event that had people dialing their friends to say, "Hey, turn on your TV and check this out." But he had to get Josh out from behind the trash can.

"Ya think?" Josh's hopes started to rise. Maybe millions of people *hadn't* seen him twitch like a helpless rag doll.

"Totally — don't worry about it," Drake said. He grabbed Josh's arm. "C'mon out."

Josh mustered his courage and stood. The minute he stepped into the café with Drake, heads turned. He had changed into his Premiere uniform — a bright red vest with a big P on the lapel — but people still recognized him from the news. Premiere customers started to whisper. Some giggled. Others snickered.

"Hey, look! It's the kid from the weather who couldn't stop twitching," said a guy in a blue-striped shirt.

"Oh, yeah! I love that guy," his friend answered. "Hey, Twitchy," he yelled.

"Hey, twitch it up!" the first guy added.

Suddenly, a dozen customers were pointing at Josh and laughing. A couple of them imitated Josh's twitch. So much for no one watching the weather.

Josh gave Drake an "I told you so" look.

Drake shrugged. "I guess people do watch the weather. Who knew?"

Josh groaned. Customers gathered around, asking Josh to twitch. Helen pushed through the crowd like a linebacker on a football field.

"Hey, hey, hey!" She sent people flying in all directions. "Make a path." Helen stood in front of Josh like a bodyguard and faced the crowd. "You leave this boy alone! Isn't it bad enough he humiliated and degraded himself on television?" she yelled.

Josh was relieved Helen was making everyone stop,

but did she have to remind everybody that he had totally embarrassed himself on television? "Thank you, Helen," he said sarcastically.

"You're welcome, Twitchy," Helen said. If anybody was going to ridicule and abuse one of her employees, it was going to be her.

"Hey!" Josh protested.

"Don't you 'hey' me. You better get to work," Helen ordered. Sure Helen was willing to protect Josh, but in the end, she was all business.

She turned to the crowd. "And you all disperse! Break it up! Move it. Move it!"

The crowd drifted away. Drake wanted to stay and cheer up Josh, but he had a talent contest to get ready for and a band waiting for him.

Josh moped over to the concession counter. He was afraid that he'd never live this down. What if people called him Twitchy for the rest of his life?

Drake had other things on his mind — beating Hewitt in the talent contest. He rehearsed with his band across the room. The drummer used silverware and the tabletop as a makeshift drum while Drake played his guitar and sang.

Hewitt watched and listened. He signaled the Choral Society with his eyes and strutted up to Drake. "Nice song, Drake," he sneered.

"Thanks, Hewitt," Drake sneered back.

"Is that what you're going to sing at the talent show?" Hewitt asked.

"Maybe."

"Doesn't matter," Hewitt said. "We're going to sing all over you."

Drake wasn't quite sure what "sing all over you" meant, but there was no way he was going to take Hewitt's threats. "You know," he said, looking Hewitt up and down. "You've got a lot of confidence for a guy in a sweater-vest."

Drake's band members cracked up. Those sweater-vests were pretty outdated.

"You want to know why I have confidence?" Hewitt tried to sound tough. "Check it." He raised his hand in the air.

"Check what?" Drake asked.

"I was about to snap," Hewitt said. Sadly, he wasn't

quite as smooth as he tried to be. He snapped his fingers, and the other members of the Choral Society surrounded him. "Five . . . Six . . . Seven . . . Eight . . ."

Drake's band laughed at the Choral Society's dorky clothes as the group launched into a song:

> I'm losing my head over you.
> Yeah, Yeah, Yeah.
> I'm losing my mind over you.
> I think I'm losing you.

But not only was their song good, their dance moves were as polished as the boy bands on MTV. A crowd gathered, totally getting into it. They cheered when the song ended. Drake and his band sat open-mouthed. When did the Choral Society learn how to do *that*?

Hewitt got right in Drake's face. "See you at the talent show, *Drake*."

Drake turned to his band, suddenly worried. "They're good," he said. Maybe his "three-peat" wasn't such a lock after all.

"Way good," the drummer agreed.

"They could beat us," added the bass player.

"We have got to rehearse," Drake said. "Now." He grabbed his guitar, and the band took off. Drake had never lost at anything before, and he wasn't about to start now.

Across the theater, Josh polished the glass on the snack counter with his head down. Maybe people would forget about the whole twitching thing if he didn't draw attention to himself. But then the guy who had first called Josh Twitchy ran up with his friend. "Hey, will you tell him if I'm doing the twitch right?"

"Huh?" Josh asked.

The guy twitched.

"That's not how he did it," his friend in the blue striped shirt said. "He did it like this." Now the friend twitched.

"No," the first guy said. "It was more like . . ." He twitched his face.

"No, like this." His friend twitched again, with his face and his shoulders.

"No it was like . . ."

The guys had a twitching contest. Josh sighed and slid down behind the snack counter. Would he have to hide out for the rest of his life?

CHAPTER SIX

Drake slept in the back of Mr. Demopoulos's geography classroom while Vanessa gave her oral report. He had been rehearsing like crazy with his band — there was *no way* they could let Hewitt and the Choral Society win first place.

No way.

And if the result of all his hard work meant sleeping through geography, it was a small price to pay.

"The country of Greece is not only the birthplace of democracy, it's given us the Olympics, baklava, and the world's earliest . . ." Vanessa said.

Drake snored softly.

Josh sat behind him. Geography was not the place to take a nap. He threw balled up pieces of notebook paper, trying to get Drake's attention. "Drake . . . Drake . . . Drake," Josh whispered.

Drake didn't move.

Josh threw three paper balls at once, hitting Drake on the back of the neck. That woke him up.

"Dude," Drake whispered. "I'm trying to sleep."

Josh rolled his eyes in disbelief. "We're in class," he answered.

"Yes, the perfect time to sleep," Drake said.

Josh gave him a blank stare. Sometimes he just didn't understand his brother. They were there to *learn*, not sleep.

"Me and the band were up all night rehearsing for the talent show," Drake explained. "I've got to get some rest." He turned around again and put his head back down on the desk.

Vanessa droned on in the background. ". . . and perhaps the most important thing that Greece has given the world are the Greek people themselves. Thank you." She sucked up to their teacher with a big smile. Everyone knew Mr. Demopoulos was Greek.

Mr. Demopoulos clapped. "Excellent report, Vanessa."

"Thank you, Mr. Demopoulos." Vanessa went back to her seat.

He admired her poster — a map of the country surrounded by pictures of the people and places of Greece. "Okay, our next oral report will be from . . ." Mr. Demopoulos checked his clipboard. "Mr. Nichols. Josh?"

Josh headed for the front of the room.

Drake grabbed his arm as he walked by. "Hey, keep it down, all right? I'm trying to . . ." Drake put his head down on his hands, letting Josh know he wanted to sleep.

Josh rolled his eyes and kept going. He put a map of Persia on the easel in the front of the room and cleared his throat.

"Persia," Josh said to the class. "What do we know about this mystery land?" Josh had practiced his oral report in front of the mirror a bunch of times and had it memorized, but standing in the front of all those kids made him nervous. He had one small facial twitch. The class laughed.

Josh kept going. Maybe if he ignored it, the twitch would stop. "Uh . . . Persia was first founded by . . ." Josh twitched some more. Now his body started jerking around — first his right side, then his left. "The Persians."

"He's twitching." Vanessa pointed and laughed.

Josh twitched even more. The class started cracking up.

Josh twitched like crazy. He looked like a dancing pumpkin in his bright orange polo shirt, but he tried to keep going. "The native language of Persia is Farsi." Then he got stuck on the word, and each time he repeated it, his head jerked to the left and more of his body got involved in the twitch. "Farsi . . . Farsi . . . Farsi . . ." The next thing he knew, his entire body was practically convulsing, just like on the news, and he didn't even want to think about the sweat stains that were forming on his shirt.

Drake sat back in his seat with a grin. He knew Josh was having a hard time, but this was just too funny to ignore. "No way I'm sleeping through this," he said.

CHAPTER SEVEN

After school, Megan kicked back on the recliner in Drake and Josh's room wearing a short sleeve purple-and-white T-shirt layered over a long sleeve purple shirt and flared black jeans. She giggled, watching the video of Josh's weatherman performance.

"It's a little warm in here," Josh said on the TV screen. Then he took off his jacket and showed the world his huge sweat stains while his whole body twitched. It was too funny!

The guys walked in. They threw their backpacks onto Josh's bed, still talking about Josh's meltdown during his oral report.

"You're overreacting," Drake said.

"I am not," Josh said. "That weather broadcast is going to haunt me for the rest of my life."

Megan laughed while she watched Josh twitch his way into full meltdown. She kept rewinding the tape to see Josh's biggest twitch.

"Megan, get out of our room," Drake said.

"Hang on," Megan said. "I just need to see this one more time." She pointed the remote control at the TV and rewound the tape, zeroing in on Josh's twitchiest moment. She cracked up. "It never gets old."

Josh turned to Drake with an "I told you so" look. Here was proof that he was right — the weather broadcast would follow him for the rest of his life. "You see?" he said.

Drake leaned down and looked right into Megan's eyes. Standing up to Megan could backfire on him, but he had to defend Josh. "You're not going to get old if you don't get out of here."

"Fine." Megan got up and went to the VCR. "It smells like boy in here anyway." She ejected the tape and started to leave the room.

"Whoa." Josh grabbed the tape. "This tape stays right here."

"Whatever." Megan shrugged. "I already put it on the Internet," she said over her shoulder as she ran out of the room.

Josh plopped on the couch with a big groan. "My

life is over. I might as well drop out of school and move to China."

Drake flipped through a guitar magazine. "They have the Internet there, too," he said. He felt badly for Josh, but sometimes it was hard to relate. It was like the guy was a giant bad luck magnet. Embarrassing situations just seemed to find Josh, no matter how hard he tried to avoid them.

"Well, that's it." Josh dropped the video on the coffee table. "I am never going up in front of people again. I'm going to live in a cave. Just me and trail mix."

It was time to change the subject; Josh had to stop thinking about the weather disaster. Drake took the remote and climbed onto his loft bed, flipping the channels. "Hey, it's the *Blues Brothers*," he said, pointing to the TV.

"So?" Josh said. What did the *Blues Brothers* have to do with Josh moving to a cave? Drake just didn't get it. He lived in a world where everything always went right — it was like the guy was a good luck magnet. He had no idea what real life — what Josh's life — was like.

"So this will cheer you up. We love the *Blues Brothers*," Drake answered.

He watched Jake and Elwood, the Blues Brothers, on screen. The Blues Brothers were squeezed into a phone booth.

Josh just stared at the TV with a sad expression. That was one of his favorite parts, and he couldn't even crack a smile.

"You're not looking very cheer-eeee," Drake said in a singsongy voice. "Here, c'mon." He turned off the TV and tossed Josh his harmonica. "Let's do our Blues Brothers routine," he said, picking up his electric guitar. "That always pumps you up." He strummed his guitar and started to sing. At this point he would try anything to get Josh out of his funk. "*Coming to you, on a dusty road.*"

He signaled Josh to take the next line.

"*Good loving,*" Josh sang miserably. "*I got a truckload.*"

Drake held the harmonica to Josh's mouth, and Josh blew a single, sad note.

"Man. You're really upset." If Josh wasn't getting into the Blues Brothers song, then he was in really bad shape.

"Yeah," Josh stood and slipped his hands into his pockets. He had no idea what to do to make himself feel better.

"You know what I'm going to do for you, man?" Drake said. "After this talent show, I'm going to help you get through this."

Josh sighed. He knew that if anyone could help him get through this, it would be his brother Drake. "Okay," he said.

"But first," Drake said, picking up his guitar with a guilty smile. "I'm going to need some time alone to rehearse." He felt badly asking Josh to leave the room, but if he didn't practice, the Choral Society dorks might win. Hewitt would never let Drake live that down.

"Sure." Josh knew the talent contest was important to Drake. He gave his brother a sad little nod and decided to go downstairs to do his homework.

The second Josh left the room, Drake grabbed the video and shoved it into the VCR. He put his feet up on the coffee table and sat back to watch Josh take his jacket off and show the world his sweat-soaked armpits, just before he launched into his biggest, most hilarious, full-body twitch. Drake smiled; it never got old.

Josh crashed back into the room.

Uh-oh! Drake jumped to his feet, and the remote control went flying across the room.

"Turn it off!" Josh yelled, and slammed the door behind him again.

CHAPTER EIGHT

Josh sat at the kitchen table with small bowls of peanuts, raisins, and other trail mix ingredients in front of him. He combined them, a handful at a time, into one big bowl. He'd had it. It was time to go underground and live out his life out in the dark.

The phone rang. He glared at it, but pushed himself up from the table and answered. "Hello?" he said. It was another prank call — a fan of Twitchy. "Yes, I'm the twitching weatherboy," he said. Then he held the phone out in front of him and shouted loudly enough to hurt the caller's eardrum. "Stop calling!" Josh slammed the phone down hard and went back to his trail mix.

Walter and Audrey came in, dressed and ready for the talent contest.

"Megan, come on!" Walter called.

"Josh," Audrey said. "Let's get going. The talent show starts in forty-five minutes."

Walter checked out the snacks on the table. "What are you making?" he asked.

"Trail mix," Josh said sadly. "For the cave I'm going to live in. Where no one can see me twitch in the darkness."

Walter and Audrey exchanged sympathetic looks.

"We understand why you're upset," Walter said.

"But you've got to come to the talent show and support your brother," Audrey added.

Josh looked at her. Was she crazy? There was no way he wanted to go back to the Premiere and be humiliated yet again.

"He'd do it for you," Audrey said.

Josh let out a big sigh. It was true. If things were reversed, Drake would be there for Josh. So Josh would have to be there for Drake. That's what brothers did. "Okay." He sighed again. "But if I have to go out in public, I'm doing it my way." He grabbed a black ski mask off the chair next to him and pulled it over his face before trudging out of the kitchen.

The Premiere theater was totally transformed for the talent show. A stage surrounded by sparkly black curtains had been set up for the performers. Glittery stars surrounded the words "Belleview Talent Contest" on the banner that hung over the stage. Movie posters had been replaced with signs for the show, and the café tables had been moved aside to make room for chairs for the audience — mostly high school kids.

An usher handed Audrey a program and did a double take when he saw Josh's ski mask.

A violinist on stage hit a sour note. The whole room cringed.

"Is that a violin?" Walter asked. He munched on a handful of Josh's homemade trail mix.

Megan covered her ears. "It sounds like a moose got hit by a car."

Audrey shushed her.

"Is Drake's band up next?" Walter asked.

Audrey checked her program. "No. It's the Choral Society."

"The dorks who performed on our porch last Christmas?" Megan asked.

"Don't say dorks," Audrey said. She thought about it for a second. "Though they were dorks."

Walter nodded. He was in full agreement on that. They were total dorks.

Audrey and Megan looked for seats. Walter hung back to talk to his son. "Josh, will you take that ski mask off. You're freaking people out," Walter said.

"No," Josh insisted. "This way, no one knows who I am."

But Josh was more recognizable than he thought. He stopped short when he heard someone yell.

"Hey, look! It's the kid from the weather who couldn't stop twitching."

"Oh, yeah!" His friend got excited. "I love that guy! Hey, Twitchy," he called to Josh.

"Twitch it up!" said the first guy.

"C'mon. Twitch," said his friend.

Josh pulled the ski mask off in despair and plodded over to his family. He really would have to go and live in a cave unless he wanted to be known as Twitchy forever.

Onstage, the violinist finally finished what was supposed to be a song. She curtsied to the audience and slunk off stage to a small smattering of polite applause. Except for her best friends, everybody else in the audience was just glad that she was finally finished.

Josh's boss, Helen, grabbed the microphone. She wore a glittery black-and-white top and black pants for the big night. "Thank you." She checked her index card. "Cookie Hancock for that wonderful rendition of the Canadian national anthem. Okay, now, please make some noise for our next act." She checked her index card again. "The Belleview Choral Society!"

Hewitt and his friends strutted onstage. They had exchanged their sweater-vests for cool vintage shirts and faded jeans. Even their hair looked great. It was like they had a total makeover. The audience clapped.

Drake and his band watched from backstage. The Choral Society was their only real competition. Drake's jaw dropped. "What happened?" he asked. "They look *cool*. Dorks aren't supposed to look cool. That's against dork rules."

"Don't worry man," the drummer answered. "They can't touch us."

"Totally," added the bass player. "Your song rocks."

Onstage, Hewitt snapped his fingers. "One, two, three . . ." The Choral Society launched into their song. But they hadn't just copied Drake's cool look; they were singing Drake's song, too.

I never thought it'd be so simple but,
I found a way, I found a way.
If you open up your mind, you'll see what's inside . . .
It's gonna take some time to realize,
But if you look inside I'm sure you'll find

Not only did their voices blend perfectly, but they had great choreography, too. No one made a mistake. And the audience loved it.

Drake watched, totally and completely horrified. "No way," he said. "No way, no way, no way."

"Dude! They stole our song," the bass player said.

"Ya think?" Drake answered.

Audrey fumed in the audience. She crossed her arms over her chest. "Those dorks stole Drake's song!" she whispered to Megan.

Megan nodded angrily. She could pick on Drake all she wanted — besides picking on Josh, it was her favorite thing to do in the world. But as far as she was concerned, everybody else had better back off.

Josh forgot about his own problems and ran backstage to help his brother. What if Drake was busy rehearsing and didn't know what was going on? "Drake! Did you notice their song sounds extremely similar to yours?"

Drake was outraged. "That *is* my song. They stole the song I wrote."

"So what are you going to do?" Josh asked.

Drake threw his arms up in the air. He was not about to give up without a fight. But right now, with this whole band waiting for him to answer Josh's question, he had no idea what to do. "We're going to have to sing something else," he said.

"What?" asked the bass player.

A guy wearing a baseball cap and a logo T-shirt walked past. He stopped short when he saw Josh. "Whoa," he said. "You're the twitchy weatherboy."

Drake had a serious problem. He didn't have time

for this distraction right now. He had to find a new song. "Dude, knock it off," Drake said.

The guy ignored Drake. "Hey listen," he said to Josh. "My dad's over there. It's his birthday. If I bring him over, would you twitch for him?"

Josh looked away with a pained expression.

The guy didn't wait for an answer. "Hey, Dad!" he called, running off to get his father.

Josh sighed. "I knew I should've stayed home." He pulled the ski mask over his face and trudged away before the guy could come back.

"Josh." Drake started to go after him. Josh was totally bummed. Josh knew his brother needed him. But his band did, too. The drummer grabbed Drake's arm.

"Focus, man," the drummer said. "What are we going to sing?"

Drake watched Josh walk away. It gave him an idea — an excellent idea. "All right, I know exactly what we're going to play."

"What?" asked his bandmates.

"Something cool," Drake answered. "I need my mom!"

The band eyed each other, confused. What in the world was Drake up to? And how could it be cool if Drake's mom had anything to do with it?

Drake ran off to find Audrey. But he didn't just need his mom. He had to get Josh on board, too.

CHAPTER NINE

Drake waited by the door, nervously checking his watch. A guy onstage did a lame juggling act. He kept dropping one of the balls.

Finally, Audrey ran in carrying two shopping bags. "Here you go," she said. "It's all here."

"Okay, thanks." Drake grabbed the bags and ran over to Josh, who was slumped in the back row, still wearing his ski mask. "Josh!" Drake grabbed his arm and pulled him to his feet.

Josh didn't look up. "No, I'm not going to twitch for your dad." Then he realized it was Drake. "Oh, hey." He pulled his ski mask off. "What's up?"

"You are." Drake answered.

"Huh?" Josh had no idea what Drake was talking about.

Drake showed him the bags. One was filled with black sunglasses, the other with two black suits, ties, and hats. "We're doing the Blues Brothers together," Drake said.

"What?" Josh looked at Drake like he had lost his mind.

"You're going to sing 'Soul Man' with me," Drake said.

"What is this, Twitch-a-palooza?" Josh opened and closed one of the bags. "You know what happens to me when I get up in front of people."

"Yeah, and it's going to keep happening if you don't get over it now," Drake said.

"Drake, I can't." Was Drake totally clueless? Josh would get up there and start twitching again. It would be a disaster.

"You want me to lose?" Drake asked.

"No," Josh said. "Of course I don't want you to —"

Drake interrupted. "C'mon, you're my brother. Brothers help brothers." He couldn't believe Josh said no, just when Drake needed him the most.

"Drake, I'm not going up there!" Josh insisted. He tried to give Drake back the bag with the suits.

Drake didn't have time for this. His band was up next, and without two Blues Brothers, the song would bomb — big time. He grabbed the bag. "Fine," Drake nodded. "But without you . . . I'm going to lose."

Josh watched Drake storm backstage. Not only had he become Twitchy, but now he had let Drake down, too.

The juggler finished his act. Helen took the stage. "And now, our final act of the evening. It's a boy very dear to my own heart." Helen looked out over the audience. Her voice rose with excitement. "So give it up for Drake Parker and his band, whose names I do not know!"

The audience went wild — especially Audrey, Walter, and Megan.

Drake stepped onstage wearing his black suit, a Blues Brothers porkpie hat, a narrow black tie, and black sunglasses. His bandmates wore sunglasses, too.

Hewitt and the Choral Society glared from the audience. They had expected Drake's band to choke, not to come back with another song.

Drake walked up to the microphone. "Thank you," he said. "We're going to do a tribute to the Blues Brothers." It would be weird to sing the song with just one brother, but at this point he was out of ideas. He turned to the band. "One, two, three, four . . ."

The band launched into "Soul Man." Drake started to sing.

Coming to you, on a dusty road

Suddenly Josh waved from the sidelines. He was dressed in his Blues Brothers suit and wearing black sunglasses. He did two back handsprings onto the stage and landed next to Drake just in time to join him on the chorus.

Soul man!

The audience went crazy as Drake and Josh sang together.

Josh forgot all about twitching. He did the same crazy dance moves as John Belushi had done in the movie, while Drake sang the next verse.

Got what I got, the hard way

Josh twisted and jumped. His dance moves got as much attention as Drake's singing. Josh danced up to Drake again to sing the chorus.

Soul man!

Helen and the rest of the audience rocked out to the music.

Josh moved across the stage, and Drake mimed throwing him a rope. Both brothers sang the next verse.

Then they did some more dance moves. Drake twirled Josh around and slipped him his harmonica. They did wild kicks while Josh played the blues, and then launched into the chorus again.

I'm a soul man . . .

The whole audience danced in their seats, singing and clapping along with the band. Josh did two more back handsprings and landed in a split just as the music ended.

The crowd went wild.

Helen rushed the stage. "Well, we have our winner!" Helen pointed. "Drake Parker!"

Drake threw his arm around Josh and grabbed the microphone. "And my brother, Josh," he shouted.

The crowd cheered.

Hewitt scowled from the sidelines. "Forget this," he said to the Choral Society. "Let's go sing some Christmas carols."

But Drake had forgotten all about Hewitt. The real victory was Josh's. Drake covered the microphone as the audience continued to cheer. "Well bro," he said to Josh. "It looks like your twitching days are over."

Josh grinned. "Looks like you just won the talent show for the second year in a row."

Out of nowhere, the same mysterious girl popped up between Drake and Josh. She wore a pink top and had a pink feather boa wrapped around her neck. "Actually, it's three years. It's a three-peat! Just like I predicted."

Drake and Josh looked at each other, then at the girl. "Who *are* you?" they asked at the same time.

"I love you. 'Bye!" she said to Drake and darted off again.

Josh watched her run away and shook his head. Maybe if he hung around with Drake long enough, pretty girls would do that for him. "It's got to be fun being you."

Drake thought about it for a second. "Yeah," he agreed.

They put their sunglasses back on and took some more bows.

Drake got his three-peat, but Josh was the night's real winner. And neither one of them could have done it without his brother.

Part Two:
Number One Fan

PROLOGUE

Josh Nichols sat on the window seat in the living room, doing his homework. "You know, I love little kids," he said.

Drake Parker hung out on the loft bed in his room. "Kids are awesome." He grabbed a blue shirt from the pile next to him.

"You know what I like best about them?" Josh asked.

Drake sniffed the shirt and threw it aside. It wasn't clean. "The coolest thing about hanging with kids?"

"They can learn a lot from me," Josh said.

"They can learn a lot from me," Drake said.

Josh looked up from his geography notes. "I used to tutor this little Portuguese boy in math. His name was Paolo."

"One time my mom made me babysit Megan and three of her friends." Drake tried a purple shirt. Still not clean.

"I was teaching him about long division." Josh remembered with a frown. "And he threw a golf club at me. A nine iron!"

"Mom told me to take the kids to a museum," Drake remembered with a grin. "But instead, I took them to ride go-carts."

"That club hit me in the eye. Bruised my retina." Josh cringed, feeling the pain all over again.

"After I gave the kids these huge cups of coffee, man, you should've seen them on those go-carts." Drake laughed.

"It was out of control!" Josh said.

"It was out of control!" Drake said.

Josh shook his head. "I complained to Paolo's father, but he just shouted at me in Portuguese."

"After the go-carts, we all piled into a cab and went to Chucky Cheddar's." Drake sniffed another shirt and made a face. Ugh! It was Josh's.

"I like tutoring . . . but I hate Paolo," Josh said.

"Ahhh . . . kids." Drake leaned back with a smile.

"Ahhh . . . kids." Josh shook his fist in the air. "Paolo!"

CHAPTER ONE

Josh poured milk into a big glass pitcher. The oven timer dinged.

"Woo-hoo!" Josh opened the oven door and checked out the cookie tray inside. It looked perfect. "Hello, s'mores!" He pulled the tray out of the oven, gazing at it with a proud smile. But his smile suddenly twisted into a grimace. "Hello, pain!" he screamed. Josh dropped the tray on the counter and plunged his hand into the pitcher of milk. Milk splashed all over the stove, the counter, and Josh's blue plaid shirt.

"Josh," Drake said, coming into the kitchen and seeing Josh's hand in the pitcher. "They usually put the prize in the cereal, not the milk."

Josh smirked at his brother and pulled his hand out of the pitcher.

Drake forgot about whatever Josh was doing with the milk when he noticed the tray. "S'mores! I love s'mores," he said.

Josh held Drake at bay with his dry hand. "Who doesn't?" he asked.

"I don't know." Drake shrugged. "S'more-haters?"

"Good point," Josh said, grabbing a towel. But he wondered if there could really be such a thing as a s'more-hater — a sandwich made of graham crackers, chocolate bars, and melted marshmallows was as close to perfect as you could get.

"So why are you making s'mores?" Drake asked.

"I'm helping Dad out with Megan's Campfire Kids meeting." Josh dried his hand.

"Dad's still a chief? I thought they kicked him out after the pinecone incident," Drake said. He chuckled, remembering the story of Walter versus nature. Let's just say the Campfire Kids didn't learn how to make a pinecone wreath that day.

Josh defended his dad. "Hey, that squirrel had it coming!" he said, pointing at his brother. Wildlife did not get the best of the Nichols men — not puppies, not chimps, and certainly not snack-stealing squirrels. Josh turned his back on Drake to get more milk out of the refrigerator.

Drake seized the opportunity and reached for a s'more. He wasn't a s'more-hater, that's for sure.

But Josh knew his brother too well. "And don't eat the s'mores . . ." Josh said, without turning around.

"Oh, I won't," Drake said, as he took a bite of one of the chocolate, graham cracker, and marshmallow treats.

". . . because I just took them out of a four hundred degree oven," Josh finished.

Now it was Drake's turn to grimace in pain. His mouth on fire, he dropped the s'more onto the tray. Then he spit the bite into his hand and scraped the burning crumbs off his tongue.

Drake reassembled the s'more on the tray before Josh could turn around and catch him.

Josh turned around and eyed Drake. Something was up. He could tell by the guilty expression on Drake's face. Drake was one of those lucky guys who was always getting away with things — but Josh recognized that look.

"Nothing," Drake said, answering the question before Josh could ask. He let his eyes drop to the tray — the s'more looked *almost* normal.

Josh was about to ask what "nothing" meant when his father, Walter, screamed from the living room. "Josh!"

"Coming," Josh said, reaching for the milk.

Walter screamed again, louder and more desperate this time. "Josh!"

Josh put an oven mitt on his sore hand, grabbed the tray of hot s'mores and the pitcher of milk, and hurried into the living room.

The Campfire Kids looked cute in their badge-covered khaki vests and raccoon-skin hats, but they were busy tying Walter to a chair. Walter couldn't move. It was the last time he would teach anybody to tie a knot.

The kids rushed to the other side of the living room when Josh came in. "Aw, Megan," Josh said. "You tied Dad to a chair?"

Megan jumped up from her spot in front of Walter's feet. Tying her dad up had been her idea, but he was the one who taught them all about knots in the first place. Weren't they supposed to practice? "Maybe," she said, focusing on the tray in Josh's hand. "Are those s'mores?" She reached for the tray.

The Campfire Kids crowded around Josh. Walter struggled to get out from under the ropes.

"Now," Josh said, holding the tray out of reach. "I have ten s'mores, and there are nine of you. So everybody gets one, and then we'll hold a raffle —"

"S'mores!" shouted Pete, one of the Campfire Kids.

The end of Josh's sentence was lost. The kids attacked, pulling him to the floor and sending the s'mores flying. Luckily he had put the pitcher of milk on the coffee table first, or that would have gone flying, too.

"Savages!" Josh yelled, crawling out from under them. "Savages! Get your s'mores, you little demons!" He jumped up, tripped over one of the kids, and fell down again. "I'm okay," he said, getting up for the second time. "I'm okay." He turned to his father. "You could have helped me," Josh said.

"I'm tied to a chair!" Walter yelled.

"Oh. Right." Josh remembered. He pulled the red nylon rope over Walter's head and away from his arms.

Walter stood, pushing the rope away and kicking it off his ankles. "Thank you," he said. Walter had thought that volunteering to be Megan's troop leader would bring the two of them closer together. But his relationship with Megan was fine — it was the rest of the Campfire Kids he couldn't handle.

Walter grabbed his chief's hat and pushed it onto Josh's head. "This is for you."

Josh straightened the hat. "What are you doing?" he asked.

"Resigning," Walter announced with frustration. Being tied up by Campfire Kids was even worse than being mocked by a peanut-eating squirrel. "You're the new Campfire Kids Chief."

"But I don't want to be —"

Walter cut him off. He pointed at Josh and yelled. "New chief!"

Josh cowered. "Yes, Daddy," he said.

Walter ran from the room without a backward glance. The Campfire Kids were too busy eating their s'mores to notice, but Josh watched him go with a nervous expression. If they tied Dad up, what would they do to Josh?

How hard could being a troop leader be, he thought. After all, they were just little kids. And he could teach them all about the camping and the outdoors. Then Josh remembered Paolo and the golf club. He shuddered, but decided to make the best of the whole deal.

Wendy, a Campfire Kid with brown hair and big brown eyes, looked around impatiently. She pulled Megan aside so no one else would hear. "Where's your brother?" Wendy asked.

"That *is* my brother." Megan pointed at Josh.

"Not him." Wendy shook her head. "Drake."

Megan looked confused. This wasn't the first time Wendy had wanted to know about Drake. "Why are you always asking about Drake?"

"He's only the cutest boy ever," Wendy said.

"Ahem?" Pete tried to get their attention. Didn't Wendy and Megan think he was the cutest boy ever?

The girls rolled their eyes and turned their backs on him.

"Don't you think Drake's adorable?" Wendy asked.

Megan thought about it for a second. When she pictured Drake, she imagined a bull's-eye in the middle of his forehead. "I think of him more as a target," Megan answered.

Josh tried to get everyone's attention now that the s'mores had been devoured. Since his dad had escaped without letting the troop know he was leaving, Josh's first official duty as chief would be to announce his new role in the troop. He would make the best of this — in fact, he would be the best Campfire Kids Chief ever. "All right. Listen up children!"

The Campfire Kids stared at him. Maybe he had more s'mores.

Josh strutted across the living room wearing Walter's hat. "I am your new Campfire Kid Chief!" Josh announced enthusiastically.

The kids made faces and eyed each other warily. This big goofball was in charge?

A girl with dark hair and a lisp looked worried. "You're our new chief?"

Josh nodded.

"Seriously?" she asked.

"That's right," Josh said with a big grin.

"I'm out." The girl dropped her raccoon hat to the floor and pushed past Josh to get to the front door. It slammed behind her.

Josh didn't have time to react. Drake ran in from the kitchen.

Wendy's eyes got wide. "It's Drake!" she whispered to Megan.

Megan rolled her eyes. What was the big deal about Drake? "I know," she said.

"Josh, you're not going to believe who just called me!" Drake held up his cell phone.

"Who called?" Josh asked. Drake was obviously pumped up.

"Star 99!" Drake answered. Drake had been hoping for this call for weeks. Star 99, a San Diego radio station, featured local songwriters every Friday night.

"You're in the Songwriter Spotlight?" Josh asked.

"Yes! I get to play live on the radio this Friday night!" Drake answered. Drake had played at parties and at high school talent contests, but this would be his first radio gig.

"Congrats," Josh said. "That's awesome, bro." *Figures*, he thought. Drake gets to play his music on the radio, and Josh gets stuck with a band of wild Campfire Kids.

But Pete wasn't impressed with Drake's news. His milk tasted funny. He pulled something out of his glass. "Gross!" he said. "There's a bandage in my milk."

Josh stared at the cut on his finger and remembered plunging his hand into the milk pitcher. "Aw, geez!"

CHAPTER TWO

Drake jammed on his guitar with his eyes closed and his headphones on, getting ready for his radio debut. He was writing a new song, and he wanted it to be perfect. He didn't see or hear one of the Campfire Kids slip into the bedroom he shared with Josh. Wendy stood next to him and stared for a few seconds. She couldn't believe she was actually in Drake's room, standing just inches from the coolest boy ever.

Drake turned and caught sight of her peering at him. "*Ahhhh!*" he screamed in surprise.

"Hi, Drake! Did I scare you?" she babbled. "What are you doing? Is that your guitar? Cool guitar!"

Drake stared at her with a confused expression. She was obviously in Megan's Campfire Kids group — he could tell from the uniform. But did he know this girl? "Who are you?" he asked.

Wendy hopped from foot to foot. "I'm Wendy!" she answered. "Well, my real name's Melissa but I hate the name Melissa so people call me Wendy."

"Okaaay," Drake said slowly. "I'm Drake. Nice to meet you." He looked down at his guitar. Was this conversation over? He had a song to finish.

Wendy started talking even faster. "We've met before. Well, sorta kinda. I saw you at the supermarket and I said, 'hi,' and you said, 'do you know where the pickles are?' and I said, 'right over there,'" Wendy pointed. "And you said, 'cool' — I wrote about it in my diary."

Drake pretended to remember. "Oh, yeah," he smiled. "Thanks."

"You want a pickle now? Because I'll go get you one. I mean it." Wendy said it as if she would fight her way through a blizzard to get a pickle for Drake.

Drake shook his head. This was getting too weird. Why was she offering to get him food? "That's okay," he said.

Wendy tried to keep the conversation going. "So what song were you playing?"

"Oh, it's a new one I'm working on," Drake said. He was always happy to talk about his music, but he really needed this girl to leave so he could get back to work. "I'm going to sing it on the radio this Friday night."

"Wow! You're going to be on the radio?" Wendy tried to think of something she and Drake had in common, so he would like her. "I *have* a radio!" Wendy nodded.

What was up with this girl, Drake wondered. He raised his eyebrows and nodded again. "Cool."

"Can I have your autograph?" Wendy asked.

Drake was even more confused. No one had ever asked him for an autograph before. "Why do you want my autograph?" he asked.

"You're only the bestest singer *ever*," Wendy said.

Drake was flattered, but surprised. "You know my music?"

"Sure. I go to the talent show every year just to see you," Wendy answered. "I even have some of your songs on CD. I listen to them when I work out." Wendy was getting impatient again. Would he give her an autograph or not? She really wanted it. "So can I have your autograph or what?"

"Uh, sure," Drake said. "I just need a pen —"

Wendy was ready. She had been planning this for days. It was the whole reason she joined Campfire Kids in the first place — a chance to get close to Megan

Parker's big brother. She whipped out a pen and shoved it in Drake's face. "Pen!" she announced.

"Thanks." Drake put down his guitar and looked around. "Okay, let's see, paper . . ." He wandered over to Josh's desk, which was much neater than his own. There were a couple of bobble-head football dolls on the desk, and the wall behind it was decorated with old license plates from around the country. "All right, here, this'll work." Drake picked up a piece of paper and used Josh's history notebook to lean on while he signed.

He talked as he autographed. "To Wendy. Love, Drake Parker," he said, handing the paper to Wendy. "There you go."

Wendy was so nervous and excited that she was wringing her hands. But she had one more thing to ask of Drake. "Want to hear a secret?" she said.

"Okaaay." Drake laughed. He thought Wendy was a cute kid, and she obviously had good taste in music. But why was she telling him her secrets?

"My dream is for you to play a song — just for me." She peered up at him through her bangs. "Will you?"

Drake didn't see any reason why not. He was

practicing anyway, and he'd love to get a reaction to his new song. "Sure, I guess. Let me just —"

Josh rushed in, cutting him off. "Wendy! Your mom's waiting for you downstairs in the car," he panted, out of breath. He had been looking all over for her, afraid he had lost a kid on his very first day as Campfire Kids Chief.

"But Drake was just about to play me a song!" she said, disappointed.

Drake smiled. "We'll do it another time, okay?" he said gently.

Wendy stared at the floor. She couldn't believe her mom showed up just when Drake was about to sing her a song.

Drake hated to see her so upset — after all, she *was* his first autograph seeker. "But here." Drake handed Wendy a shiny, red guitar pick.

Wendy's face lit up. "Your guitar pick?" Wendy smiled. "You're giving me *this?*"

"Yeah." Drake laughed, a little embarrassed. "For my number one fan."

"Yay!" Wendy said, closing her fist around the guitar pick.

Wendy's mother blew the car horn.

"Well, I better get going. 'Bye, Drake." She hurried out, stopping at the door to show Josh her autograph. "Look! Drake signed this for me."

Josh took the paper and turned it over. He waved it in Drake's face. "On the back of my picture of Grammy?" he asked.

Drake shrugged.

Wendy tugged the picture out of Josh's hand and ran downstairs.

CHAPTER THREE

Josh led the Campfire Kids into the Premiere's lobby, wearing his dad's khaki chief vest over a blue flannel shirt, cargo shorts, and his raccoon hat. He waved a yellow Campfire Kids flag in the air.

"What's up, bro?" Josh waved to Drake, who was hanging out in the café, and then turned to his troop. "Campfire Kids! Huddle up!"

"So, what movie are we seeing?" Liza, a Campfire Kid with blond hair, asked.

"We're not seeing a movie. We're here to learn about wilderness navigation," Josh said proudly. He had stayed up late the night before, studying his chief's guidebook, so he could teach his troop what to do if they got lost in the woods.

The Campfire Kids all groaned at the same time. They wanted to see a movie, not listen to Josh lecture them about life in the wilderness.

Pete made a face. "You're the worst," he said to Josh.

"Thank you, Pete," Josh said sarcastically. He was

here to teach these kids something important — how to find their way out of the woods alive — not see a movie. "Now, what would you do if someone dropped you off, all alone, in the middle of nowhere?"

He looked from blank face to blank face. No answer.

Megan stepped up. "I'd call Mom on my cell phone," she said.

"Say you don't have your cell phone?" Josh said.

Megan looked at Josh like he was a total goofball. "I always have my cell phone," she said.

Josh started to stress. Megan wasn't making this easy. "Your battery's dead," he said.

Megan had an answer. "I always carry a spare battery."

Josh lost it. He was trying to demonstrate how to stay alive in the wilderness, and Megan was focusing on her stupid cell phone. "It's broken!" he yelled. "It fell in a lake! A bear ate it! The point is you're lost." He waved his finger in Megan's face. "And all you have is a compass and a topographical map of the region!"

Okay, now Megan had proof that Josh was a complete goofball. "So I have a compass and a topographical map, but I don't have a cell phone?" she asked sarcastically. Like that would ever happen.

Josh was totally frustrated. *Let them stay lost in the woods,* he thought. *Let squirrels steal their snacks.* "That tears it!" He pointed to the ticket booth. "We're seeing a movie!"

The Campfire Kids cheered. Megan gave her friend Liza a high five.

The rest of the troop followed Josh to the ticket booth, but Wendy looked over her shoulder and saw Drake sitting at a table with a girl from school. She marched over to Drake's table, her hand on her hip.

Drake and Larissa drank their sodas and talked. They didn't notice Wendy standing right next to them.

Drake and Larissa giggled and flirted as they ate french fries.

Wendy cleared her throat. *"Ahem."*

They didn't hear her.

"Ahem," she said again, louder this time.

"Wendy?" Drake looked confused. Why was this girl always sneaking up on him?

"Who's she?" Wendy pointed at Larissa.

"Oh. This is my date, Larissa," Drake said.

Larissa smiled. "Hi."

Wendy stared at her for a moment — she took in Larissa's black skirt and funky top, then grabbed a chair from the next table and set it down with an angry bang. "So, Larissa, what's your favorite song of Drake's?" Wendy asked as she sat.

"Um, I didn't know Drake wrote songs." Larissa turned to Drake with a shy smile. "I'd love to hear some."

Drake was about to answer, but Wendy interrupted, determined to get rid of Larissa. "I bet you would," she said. "Look what Drake gave me." She held up the guitar pick. "It's his guitar pick. What'd he give you?"

"Uh, nothing?" Larissa said. She was still smiling, but starting to wonder what was going on.

Wendy nodded with satisfaction. "Interesting."

Drake had to jump in here. He didn't need Wendy messing things up with Larissa. "Uh, Wendy, we're kind of on a date here. Shouldn't you be with Josh and the —"

Wendy ignored him. The music thing hadn't worked. Maybe insulting Drake's date would do the trick. "Wow, Larissa. That's a lot of food."

Larissa stopped smiling. "Excuse me?"

"Is that all for you?" she asked.

Drake had to stop Wendy before she really insulted Larissa. "Wendy," he said in a tone of voice that really meant "stop, what do you think you're doing?"

"What?" Wendy said, fluttering her eyelashes with an innocent expression. "I think it's nice that Larissa doesn't worry about her figure."

Larissa was really getting mad now. "For your information," Larissa said, "I go to the gym four times a week."

Wendy moved on to something else. "There's a pimple on your chin," she said.

Horrified, Larissa covered her chin with her hands. "Drake!"

Drake had had enough. "All right. It's time for you to go," he said to Wendy.

"Yeah, seriously," Larissa agreed.

Wendy raised her hands in surrender. "Okay, fine." She focused on Larissa. "Enjoy your *feast*." Her tone of voice changed when she turned to Drake. "'Bye, Drake," she said sweetly.

Larissa narrowed her eyes and watched her leave. "Can you believe her?" Larissa asked.

Drake eyed the baskets of food on the table. To be completely honest, Larissa's snack order had cost him half of Josh's allowance. Wendy had been out of line, but she was his number one fan, and he thought he should at least try to defend her. "It is a lot of food," he said.

Now Larissa was as unhappy with Drake as she had been with Wendy.

CHAPTER FOUR

Josh was fluffing his pillows and making his bed when Drake rushed in waving a notebook. "Josh. I have a problem," he said.

Josh held his hand up, keeping Drake at a safe distance. "Does it itch?" Josh asked, nervously eyeing Drake's red T-shirt. You could never be too careful when it came to itching.

Itch? What was Josh thinking? "No!" Drake yelled. "My problem is Wendy, your little Forest Fire Kid."

"Oh, your number one fan," Josh teased.

"Yeah. She's obsessed with me," Drake said. "Today she verbally assaulted my friend." Drake got angry again, remembering the way Wendy insulted Larissa. If this kept up, she'd do some serious damage to his social life. But that wasn't all. He had more proof of Wendy's obsession. "Look — Megan found her notebook."

Josh took the book and looked at the cover. "Aw, she wrote 'Drake and Wendy' over and over." He laughed. It was cute. What was Drake so freaked out about? Josh flipped through the notebook. "Hey! If you flip the pages really fast there's a little cartoon of you two walking and holding hands."

Drake looked over Josh's shoulder. "Oh yeah. I wonder how she —" He cut himself off, knocking the notebook out of Josh's hands. "Oh, this is not the time for animation! Wendy is *obsessed* with me."

"You're exaggerating," Josh said. Drake was freaked out about a little crush. It certainly didn't call for notebook throwing.

"Oh yeah?" Drake said. "Here. Check out her answering machine." He walked across the room and grabbed the phone. He dialed Wendy's number and put the phone on speaker.

Her outgoing message played: "Hi, this is Wendy. Drake's not here right now, but if he were, that would be so awesome! I love you Drake!" she squealed. Then her voice got more serious and businesslike: "Please leave a message."

Drake crossed his arms over his chest and looked at Josh. The message proved that Wendy was obsessed. "See what I mean?" he said.

"So, she's got a crush on you. It's cute," Josh said.

He plopped down on the couch and put his feet up on the coffee table. "When I was her age, I had a crush on Oprah."

Drake did a double take. "Oprah?" he asked. Wasn't she, like, fifty years old? Okay, Josh was definitely weirder than he thought.

"She's an inspiration!" Josh yelled. "Dude, don't worry about Wendy. This week she loves you, next week she'll love —"

Drake made a face. "Oprah?" he teased.

Josh sat up. "Don't mock me!"

Drake sighed. "Fine. I just hope you're right."

"I am right. And you should really give Oprah a chance; she gives great —"

Josh was cut off by the sound of something tapping on glass. He and Drake looked at each other, confused.

"What's that?" Drake stood up and looked around the room.

"I don't know." Josh stood, too.

They headed for the window. Drake pulled up the shade. Wendy was leaning against the house on a ladder, holding a big jar.

Drake screamed. "Wendy! What are you doing here?"

She showed him her jar. "I brought you some pickles!" Wendy had read that the way to a man's heart is through his stomach, and she knew Drake liked pickles.

Drake lowered the shade, threw his arms up in the air, and gave Josh an "I told you so" look.

Wendy wasn't about to let a silly window shade come between her and Drake. "They're vertically sliced for sandwiches!" she shouted.

CHAPTER FIVE

Drake paced around the living room. He was wearing his "Be Reasonable. Demand the Impossible" T-shirt, but Drake didn't feel reasonable. As far as he was concerned, Wendy's crush was out of control.

"This thing with Wendy has got to stop!" he said. He stopped pacing for a second and tried to figure out what Josh was doing. Josh poured peanuts into a metal canister. His Campfire Kids Chief camping guide was open in front of him. "What are you doing with those nuts?" Drake asked.

"Protecting them from bears," Josh said with a satisfied grin. "See?" He put the top on the canister and locked it. "A bear's not smart enough to open this latch."

"Cool. Hey, give me some nuts," Drake said.

Josh pulled on the latch. It didn't open. He turned it, then pulled again. It wouldn't budge. He twisted and pushed and pulled, but he still couldn't open the canister. He wrestled with it — no luck.

Drake watched, amused. "You want me to call a bear to help you?"

Josh changed the subject. "All right, so what are you going to do about Wendy?"

"I'm just going to have to tell her to leave me alone," Drake said. He stood and marched toward the door, grabbing his denim jacket. He was determined to put an end to this crazy crush. "I'm going to her house right now. Be back in an hour."

Drake opened the door to find Wendy standing on the doorstep, smiling.

"Hi, Drake." She skipped past him. "I'm coming in."

"I see that," Drake said. Wendy twirled. She was wearing pink capri pants and a T-shirt. Drake's jaw dropped when he saw what was on her T-shirt. "Is that my picture on your shirt!?" he asked.

"Yeah." Wendy struck a pose so he could get a better look at himself. "How cute are you?" Wendy said.

"Why are my eyes closed?" Drake asked.

"I took it while you were sleeping," Wendy grinned.

"Riiiight," Drake said slowly. "Um, we need to talk."

"Cool." Wendy was super excited. Drake wanted to talk — to her! "I could talk to you forever," she said.

"Great." Drake led Wendy to the couch. "Sit down."

"Hey, Josh," Wendy said. "I made a Drake T-shirt special for you." She pulled a huge T-shirt out of her backpack.

Josh put the locked canister down and held the T-shirt up in front of him. It was big enough for two or three Joshes. "Is this for me," he asked, sarcastically, "or a *sports utility vehicle?*"

Wendy had already turned back to Drake.

"So, Wendy . . ." Drake said, nervously. He didn't want to have to deal with Wendy's obsession anymore, but he didn't want to hurt her feelings either.

"So, Drake . . ." Wendy answered, waiting.

"Relationships are very complex," Drake explained.

"Oh, I know. I watch Oprah," Wendy nodded.

Josh chimed in dreamily. "Isn't she inspirational?"

"Yeah. Have you seen the one where the girl gives up her whole career just to let her husband go to medical school?" Wendy asked.

"Oh yeah! Then she started her own cookie

company!" Josh got carried away. Oprah's stories were always so encouraging!

"I know!" Wendy said excitedly. "I love that —"

"Guys, guys, guys!" Drake shouted. "I'm trying to say something here."

Josh and Wendy stopped talking.

"So, Wendy . . ." Drake said slowly, still not sure how to get his point across without making Wendy feel bad.

"Drake . . ." Wendy moved toward him and stood with a hopeful smile.

Drake stood, too, and backed away. "Look, I really appreciate that you like me and you think my music is cool," Drake said.

Wendy jumped in. "My dream is for you to play a song, just for me." *Was today the day?* she wondered.

"I know, I know." Drake put his hand on her shoulder and they sat on the couch again. "But . . . look. I think that maybe you've been paying a little too much attention to me lately."

Wendy's forehead crinkled in confusion. She didn't understand. "Did I do something wrong?"

Drake struggled to come up with a reason that wouldn't hurt Wendy's feelings. "No, no. It's not you.

It's me," he said. "You know, I just need . . . my space. Can you understand that?" Drake wasn't even sure he understood that, but he hoped it would work.

"Totally!" Wendy said, cheerfully.

"Really?" Drake was confused. This was too easy.

"Sure. I soooo get it." Wendy bounced to her feet.

"Oh, that's awesome," Drake said, totally relieved. "Look, I really appreciate you being so cool about this."

"Not a problem." Wendy took the nut canister, opened it, and popped a handful of peanuts in her mouth. "Yum. Well, I'd better go. I've got to pack for tomorrow night's campout." She closed the lid and handed the canister back to Josh. "See you," Wendy said, and breezed out the front door.

Josh struggled to open the canister again. He turned and pulled, then he pushed and turned. He yanked on the handle with all his might. It wouldn't budge.

Drake laughed. "Seriously, dude. I can call a bear."

The next morning, Drake and Josh straggled into Mr. Demopoulos's geography class a few seconds before the bell rang. They were still talking about the crazy theory Drake proposed in biology.

"Yeah, but if that were true," Josh said, "then fish would have feet, which they don't."

"Yeah, but —" Drake came to a dead stop when they saw the door to the classroom.

It was covered with hundreds of flyers about Drake's radio performance. And they all had the same photo as the one Wendy had transferred onto her T-shirt — Drake sleeping!

"Holy snot!" Drake said. He pulled one of the flyers off the door with a look of horror on his face and read it to Josh. "Catch Drake Parker, the bestest singer in the whole world, performing live this Friday night on Star 99's Songwriter Spotlight." Drake waved the flyer in Josh's face. "Josh, do you realize what your little Campfire Kid has done?"

Josh checked out the classroom. "Oh, I think *everyone* realizes it," he said.

There were hundreds of flyers, posted all over the walls, on the blackboard, even on the trash can, and Mr. Demopoulos's desk. No one could possibly miss them. Drake looked around in shock.

"Gee, Drake," a girl mocked. "Are you by any chance going to be on the radio this Friday? Just curious."

The other kids laughed.

"Guys, yeah. I'm going to be on the radio Friday, but I had nothing to do with these flyers!" Drake pulled some off the walls and crumpled them into a ball.

"Yeah, right," somebody yelled from across the room.

"Sure you didn't," said another guy.

Mr. Demopoulos came in, checking his watch and cutting off the rest of the comments. "All right, class," he said. "Let's take our seats. Thank you. There's a lot to cover —" He did a double take when he caught sight of the flyers, especially the ones that had been strung like a border around his desk. But it was time for class. He ignored them. "Now today we'll be discussing why there is no East Virginia. When we take a look at the map, we'll see." Mr. Demopoulos pulled down the map over the blackboard in the front of the room. There was a huge version of Wendy's flyer about Drake's radio gig posted over the map of the United States.

The class cracked up. Drake slid down in his seat and buried his head in his hands, ready to die of embarrassment. Mr. Demopoulos couldn't ignore *that*!

CHAPTER SIX

The Campfire Kids gathered in Megan's living room after school, watching the rain pour outside. Josh had all the camping equipment ready to be carried into the backyard. He wanted to really rough it in the woods, but since none of the Campfire Kids knew how to find their way out of the wilderness without a cell phone, he couldn't take the chance. What if someone got lost? The backyard would have to do for tonight.

"All right, Campfire cadets," Josh said, checking his watch. "Tonight's campout will begin in oh-five minutes."

"Why can't you just say five minutes?" Pete asked.

"You drop and give me twenty!" Josh commanded.

Pete stood. "Don't you mean 'oh-twenty'?" he sneered.

Everyone laughed.

Josh sighed. "Just be ready in five minutes," he said, heading into the kitchen.

Wendy tapped Megan on the shoulder. "Hey, Megan. You know that one day I'll be your sister-in-law?"

Megan laughed. "What are you talking about?"

"When Drake and I get married," Wendy said, showing her Drake's guitar pick. As far as she was concerned, it was as good as an engagement ring. Hadn't Drake told Megan about the two of them?

"Why would Drake marry you?" Pete asked with a sneer.

"Because he likes me. He gave me his guitar pick to prove it." Wendy waved the pick in Pete's face. "And look at this!" Wendy whipped out the autograph Drake had given her.

Megan unrolled the paper in confusion. "A picture of Josh's grandmother?" she asked.

"No," Wendy said impatiently. "The other side."

Megan flipped it over. Wendy pointed to Drake's signature. "See. Love, Drake. *Looove*."

The front door flew open. Lightning and thunder crashed outside. Drake marched right up to Wendy.

Wendy was thrilled. She'd show Pete. "Hi, Drake."

"Don't talk. Just listen," Drake said.

Wendy looked at him innocently. "Baby, what's wrong?"

Drake waved a flyer in her face. "Do you know how much trouble your little flyers caused me? Everyone in my entire school made fun of me today. Because of *you!*" Drake yelled.

"They just don't understand our relationship," Wendy said.

Drake was too angry and embarrassed to worry about Wendy's feelings this time. "We don't have a relationship! You get it?" he yelled. "I'm not going to sing a song for you, and I'm not your boyfriend. I'm not even your friend." Drake stormed out of the room, slowing down only long enough to yell over his shoulder. "So just leave me alone."

Wendy stared at the floor, trying not to cry. She had just wanted everyone to know how great Drake's music was. She thought she was doing a good thing for him, and now he hated her for it.

Pete poked fun at her. "So when's the wedding?" he mocked.

Everyone laughed, except for Megan. She watched

Wendy run out of the room. Maybe Drake had a right to be mad, but she hated to see Wendy look so sad.

Megan turned to Pete, her hands on her hips. "That wasn't nice. Funny, but not nice," she said.

Pete shrugged. "Who said I was nice?" he asked.

CHAPTER SEVEN

Josh paced in front of his troop, his arms crossed over his chest. He took his responsibility seriously. Very seriously. First they didn't want to learn about wilderness navigation, and now they didn't want to go camping — just because it was raining. "Okay. I'm disappointed in you for not braving the outdoors during a gentle rain shower."

Thunder boomed outside. Lightning flashed a second later.

"However," Josh continued, ignoring the sound of the rain pounding against the window, "we can still rough it right here." He pointed to the tent he had set up in the middle of the living room.

Pete spoke for the whole troop. "Look, man, I know this means a lot to you. But we're not into this whole Campfire Kids thing."

"Yeah," Liza agreed. "We just joined so we could hang out with our friends and eat free food."

"Why do you have to ruin it?" Pete added.

The rest of the troop agreed. "Yeah, yeah. Why do you have to ruin it?"

Ruin it?! Josh was doing his best to be a great Campfire Kids Chief. What a bunch of ungrateful little brats.

Megan jumped off the couch and hollered for attention. "Guys, guys!" The troop quieted. "Look, Josh is a goof. We all know that. But we joined the Campfire Kids and I think we owe it to Josh to learn something about camping," Megan said.

Josh grinned, relieved that someone wanted to learn something. He hadn't been studying his chief's guidebook for nothing. He had a lot of important wilderness skills to pass on to the troop.

"Josh," Megan continued, "please show us the proper use of this tent."

Josh nodded happily and moved toward the tent. "I'll be glad to. Now the cool part about this tent is that it'll keep any kind of bug out." He stepped inside. "Plus it's weatherproof."

As soon as Josh was inside the tent, Megan turned to Liza. "Give me the lock," she said.

Liza tossed the lock. Megan caught it, zipped

the tent, and locked Josh inside in one smooth move.

"So whether it's cold or it's rainy, you can stay dry." Josh pushed against the side of the tent. "Hey! What's going on? I think I'm locked in here."

The Campfire Kids cheered.

Megan took charge. "All right!" she said. "Now we're going to have a *real* campout."

"Say what?" Josh asked in a high, scared voice. He pushed against the side of the tent again, then the front.

Megan ignored him. It was time to get this party in gear. "You!" She pointed to Liza. "Start making s'mores. "You!" she ordered another girl. "Get the video games."

Pete was ready to take on any task.

"You!" Megan told him. "Order some pizza."

Pete pumped his arms in the air and then grabbed the phone. "I'm on it."

The Campfire Kids cheered again. But not everybody was happy. Wendy sat by herself with her chin in her hands, as gloomy as the weather.

"Wendy?" Megan sat next to her. "You want to come help us make s'mores?" she asked, gently.

Wendy shook her head sadly. "No thanks."

"C'mon," Megan said. "Drake was just upset. He didn't mean that stuff he said."

"Yeah he did," Wendy said in a sad little voice. "I just want to be alone."

Megan felt badly for Wendy, but she did what her friend asked and left her alone. She headed into the kitchen to help with the s'mores.

The tent was perfectly still as Josh strained to hear what was going on in the living room. "Um, could someone let me out of here?" Josh yelled. He punched the sides of the tent. "I hate camping, too." No one responded. He started shaking the tent violently. "I'm claustrophobic. I would like a s'more." The Campfire Kids kept ignoring him. Finally Josh screamed at the top of his lungs. *"Get me out of here!"*

CHAPTER EIGHT

Drake hung out in the waiting area at the radio station, ready to go on. Musicians milled around, rehearsing. All of them practiced different songs. Drake focused on the DJ's voice coming over the speakers.

". . . your host on Star 99 Songwriter Spotlight. That is Star 99 Songwriter Spotlight coming to you every . . ."

Drake tuned his guitar and reached into the pocket of his black shirt for his guitar pick. Uh oh, did he forget to bring one? "Do you have an extra pick?" he asked the girl with the guitar next to him.

She checked her pockets and shook her head.

Sidney, the radio station's manager came into the waiting room. "Kim," he said to the guitarist. "You're up next."

Drake checked the pockets of his jeans, looking for a pick. He didn't find one, but he did find a handmade card. It was yellow with hearts and flowers drawn on the front. *What's this?* he wondered. It wasn't Megan's style, but it was the kind of goofy thing Josh would do — make him a card to wish him luck on the radio. Drake's stomach sank when he opened the card and saw who it was from.

"Dear Drake," he read. "I'm sorry I made you mad. I just wanted to be your number one fan. I won't bother you ever again. Wendy."

He turned the card over. Wendy had taped the red guitar pick to the back. That made him feel even worse. All Wendy did was enjoy his music, and he had yelled at her in front of all her friends.

A girl wearing bright pink pants and a T-shirt with a picture of a fairy on the front watched Drake's face as he read the card. "Something's bothering you," she said.

"How do you know?" Drake slipped the card back into his pocket.

"It's a woman," she said. "Isn't it?"

"Kind of," Drake nodded. "A little woman."

The girl fixed her eyes on Drake. "Go to her," she said.

"Go to her?" What did that mean? Drake wondered. This girl was a little dramatic.

"Fix it," the girl said.

"Why should I fix it?" After all, he told himself, Wendy had embarrassed him in front of his whole school. That was the kind of thing that happened to Josh, not to Drake. He was still getting over the trauma. So then why did he keep focusing on Wendy's sad face?

"Because you know you should," the girl said seriously.

"How do *you* know I know I should?" Drake asked, confused.

"Because if you didn't know you know you should, I'd have no way of knowing what I obviously know." She shrugged and picked up her trumpet. "Even if I shouldn't."

Sidney came out into the waiting room again. "Leah, you're up next," he said to the girl.

Leah headed for the door. Drake grabbed her arm. "Wait," he said. "Who are you?"

"A friend. A conscience." Leah held up her trumpet. "A trumpeteer." She blew one short blast on her trumpet, and then went inside the control room to play her song.

She was right. Drake's conscience had been telling him to fix things with Wendy all night — ever since he got over being so mad at her. The sad look on her face when Drake told her to leave him alone haunted him. So what if she had embarrassed him at school? After all, she was just a kid. How many dumb things had he done as a kid? He said horrible things to her in front of all of her friends when all she wanted to do was be his number one fan.

Drake caught up with Sidney. "Hey, excuse me," Drake said.

"You're on after the rapper," Sidney said, checking his clipboard.

"Yeah, um, something came up that I need to take care of," Drake said. "Is there any way we could reschedule this?"

"I could try," Sidney said, "but I can't guarantee it. You sure you can't stick around?"

Drake hated to give up his chance to sing on the radio, but Wendy's face loomed in front of him again and he heard Leah's voice telling him to fix it. "No, this is important," Drake said. "Thanks." He ran for the door.

"Hey," Sidney called.

Drake stopped short. Was Sidney ready to reschedule? "Yeah?" Drake asked.

"Is it a woman?" Sidney asked.

Why did everyone ask him that?! "Sort of," Drake yelled over his shoulder, as he rushed out.

CHAPTER NINE

The Campfire Kids party was in full swing. There were snacks and empty pizza boxes all over the living room. Megan was having a three-way video game contest while Pete and Liza hung out in the kitchen, making more s'mores.

Wendy sat at a table by herself, her chin in her hands. She had a sick, sad feeling in her stomach, and she couldn't even pretend to smile.

"Will somebody turn up the radio," Megan said. "I think Drake is going to be on next."

"Hey, Wendy," Pete said meanly. "Don't you want to come listen to your future husband sing you a song?"

Liza laughed. Wendy looked away.

They all stopped to listen to the disc jockey. "Okay, our next songwriter performing tonight is San Diego's own Drake Parker."

"Hey!" Megan called. "Drake's on!" She jumped up and ran to the radio.

The kids gathered around the radio — everyone except Wendy.

"Whoa," the DJ said. "We got a flag on the play, here. I've just been told Drake Parker cancelled, so we're going to move on to our next performer, Jay Demopoulos, with his song 'I Feel Pretty — Greek.'"

Megan turned the radio off, disappointed. She wanted to hear Drake on the radio.

Suddenly Drake walked in looking for Wendy, determined to fix things.

"Drake, what are you doing here?" Megan asked.

Josh's voice came from inside the tent. He had grown hoarse asking the Campfire Kids to let him out, and then gave up completely. "How come you're not on the radio?"

"Because I —" Drake looked around. "Was that Josh? Where is he?" Drake asked.

"Forget him," Megan said. "Why aren't you on the radio?"

"Because." Drake took his guitar out of the case and crossed the room to where Wendy was sitting. "Hi, Wendy."

"Hi," she said sadly.

"So, you still want me to play you a song?" Drake asked.

Wendy was confused. Just a little while ago, Drake was telling her that he wasn't her friend. He told her to leave him alone. "For me?" she asked.

Drake smiled. "Just for you."

Wendy didn't smile back. "But what about all that stuff you said? I thought you hated me."

"How could I hate my number one fan?" Drake said. He launched into his new song — just for Wendy — while the rest of the Campfire Kids gathered around.

Wendy smiled for the first time since Drake yelled at her. A shiver ran up her spine. Drake was singing a song, just for her.

Thunder and lightning boomed and crackled outside, but to Wendy it seemed like fireworks on the Fourth of July. Her secret dream was coming true. Wendy realized that she and Drake weren't going to get married, but he was singing a song just for her. And telling her he was her friend. It was amazing! She would never forget this as long as she lived.

Wendy leaned forward with a big smile on her face.

She didn't want to miss one note of the music, one word of the lyrics. She looked over her shoulder to make sure the other kids were listening, too.

Drake finished the song. The Campfire Kids broke into applause. Wendy had a huge smile on her face.

"So, what'd you think?" Drake asked.

Wendy jumped up to hug him. "Yay," she said.

Drake held out his guitar pick. "I want you to keep this, okay?"

Wendy smiled even bigger and took the pick. "Double yay."

Drake put his guitar down. Singing to an audience of one made him feel better than singing to thousands of people on the radio would have. The haunting image of Wendy's sad face had been replaced with her beaming smile. "All right, kids! Who wants to go to Chucky Cheddar's?" he asked.

"I love Chucky Cheddar's!" Pete yelled.

The kids cheered and ran to the front door, following Drake. He was right all along, hanging with kids was cool.

The front door closed behind them. Josh was alone. He peered out of the tent's window. "Hey! *I* want to go to Chucky Cheddar's!" he called. "C'mon. Let me out!" The tent lurched in the direction of the door. Josh strained to hear what was going on in the room. It was silent. Had they left him home alone?

"Drake? Megan?" he called. "Could I just get some water?"

The tent lurched some more, moving in the direction of the door. It was like tutoring Paolo all over again, but at least getting locked in a tent wasn't as bad as getting whacked in the eye with a golf club. Still, they had to let him out — and soon.

"You know there's no bathroom in here," Josh yelled. "That's a problem!"

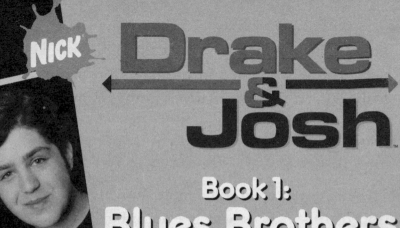